To: _____

From: _____

In memory of my parents, who shone the light of love on me,
and of my Sunday school teacher, Alice Tongue,
who taught me this spiritual —C.B.W.

To my family —T.A.

Crown Books for Young Readers
An imprint of Random House Children's Books
A division of Penguin Random House LLC
1745 Broadway, New York, NY 10019
penguinrandomhouse.com
rhcbooks.com

Library of Congress Cataloging-in-Publication Data is available upon request.
ISBN 978-0-593-80575-6 (hardcover)—ISBN 978-0-593-80576-3 (lib. bdg.)—ISBN 978-0-593-80577-0 (ebook)

The text of this book is set in 16-point Corporative Soft.
The illustrations were created digitally using Procreate on an iPad Pro.

Manufactured in China
10 9 8 7 6 5 4 3 2 1

The authorized representative in the EU for product safety and compliance is Penguin Random House Ireland, Morrison Chambers, 32 Nassau Street, Dublin D02 YH68, Ireland, https://eu-contact.penguin.ie.

LET IT SHINE!

A CELEBRATION OF YOU

Inspired by the Spiritual "This Little Light of Mine"

Carole Boston Weatherford • Tequitia Andrews

Crown Books for Young Readers New York

This little light of mine, I'm gonna let it shine.
This little light of mine, I'm gonna let it shine.
This little light of mine, I'm gonna let it shine.

LET IT SHINE

LET IT SHINE

LET IT SHINE

When you were a little one,
your light was just a spark.
Your loved ones guided you
through danger and the dark.
Beaming with such promise,
you were meant to make your mark.

LET IT SHINE
LET IT SHINE
LET IT SHINE

This little light was lit
long before you were born.
Saints paved the way for you
in shoes old and worn.

This lamp's been a beacon
through struggle and storm.

Climbing high on shoulders
as strong as they are wide,
in footsteps of your elders,
you have hit your stride.

The warmth you feel inside you
is your family's pride.

LET IT SHINE, LET IT SHINE, LET IT SHINE

This little light reflects
an everlasting flame—
hope that was passed down to you
by those who overcame.

ROSA PARKS

7053

This special moment's yours,
so own the joy you've earned.
You kept pressing on
all the while that you yearned.

Your badge of triumph
into history now is burned.

Dream big and keep the faith,
and dare to be bold.
Find determination
deep down in your soul.
The gift you have within you
is as good as gold.

LET IT SHINE

LET IT SHINE

Let it shine

When the blues blow in
and try to hold you down,
ride on wings of heroes
who wouldn't be turned around.

REV. MARTIN
LUTHER KING JR.

SHIRLEY CHISHOLM

HARRIET TUBMAN

FREDERICK DOUGLASS

You are a bright twinkle
in the universe's crown.

LET IT SHINE

LET IT SHINE

LET IT SHINE

Follow the North Star,
and you will then grow wise.
Keep your sights set high.
Aim your eyes on the prize.

You're a blazing comet
soaring through the skies.

LET IT SHINE

LET IT SHINE

LET IT SHINE

Wonder, strive, and learn;
keep growing all life long.
Trust your little light,
and then you can't go wrong.
That little light is like
a never-ending song.

You can make a difference
if you make a vow.
Listen to that little light.
Ask: Why? And how?

Give both praise and thanks
before you take your bow.

LET IT SHINE, LET IT SHINE, LET IT SHINE

Celebrate. Let's celebrate.
The race has just begun.
Press forward. Lift the torch.
Ready, get set . . . run!
Your future is so bright—
bright as the noonday sun.

That little light of yours, you gotta let it shine.
Every day you strive, you are gonna shine.
Everywhere you go, you are gonna shine.

LET IT SHINE, LET IT SHINE, LET IT SHINE!

Author's Note

Dear Readers,

Let It Shine! expands the lyrics of "This Little Light of Mine," an American spiritual that is best known as a beloved children's tune. The song's origins are unknown, but it shares characteristics of African American spirituals, suggesting roots in enslavement. Although not outwardly religious, the lyrics could allude to the Bible verses Matthew 5:14–16.

Today, church choirs and classrooms around the world sing "This Little Light of Mine." The simple verses affirm that everyone has something valuable to share.

With lyrics made for improvisation, "This Little Light of Mine" also speaks to the masses. During the Civil Rights Movement, the song sustained protesters when they were attacked, arrested, or jailed. Voting rights activist Fannie Lou Hamer, known for speeches *and* for singing, declared "This Little Light of Mine" as a favorite.

I first learned the song in Sunday school at Union Memorial Methodist Church in Baltimore. And when I pondered writing a book to mark milestones and achievements, I could not get "This Little Light of Mine" out of my head. I offer these new lyrics as a celebration of awe-inspiring individuality and as a testament to achievement against the odds. Remember: The light is not just a lamp within but also a torch to pass on.

Carole Boston Weatherford

Timeline

1925: A poetry book by Edward G. Ivins includes the line "this little light of mine."

1933: The song is first sung at an African Methodist Episcopal (AME) church conference in Helena, Montana.

1934: Folklorists John and Alan Lomax produce the earliest known recording of the song—a rendition by a Texas prison inmate.

1940s: The first published arrangement of the song appears in a hymnal.

1960s: The song becomes an anthem for the Civil Rights Movement.

Noted Artists Who Have Recorded the Song

Ray Charles (reworking it as "This Little Girl of Mine," 1955)

Sister Rosetta Tharpe (1960)

The Kingston Trio (1962)

Pete Seeger (1962)

Odetta (1963)

Sam Cooke (1964)

Mahalia Jackson (1992)

Aretha Franklin (2006)

Bruce Springsteen (2007)

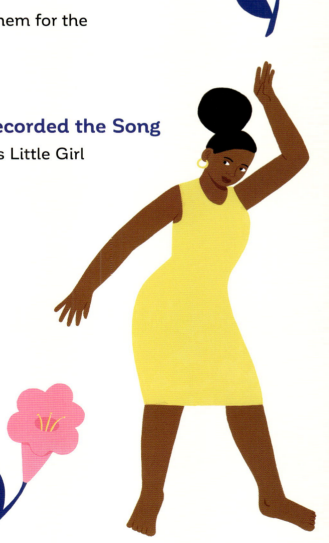